MW01611346

BOOK ANALYSIS

By Isabelle Bousquette

I Know Why the Caged Bird Sings

by Maya Angelou

Bright
≡Summaries.com

MAYA ANGELOU   9

I KNOW WHY THE CAGED BIRD SINGS   13

SUMMARY   17

Life in Stamps
Leaving Stamps
San Francisco

CHARACTER STUDY   23

Marguerite
Bailey Jr.
Momma

ANALYSIS   29

Autobiography vs. fiction
Parenthood
Oppression

FURTHER REFLECTION   37

FURTHER READING   41

MAYA ANGELOU

AMERICAN POET AND MEMOIRIST

- **Born in St. Louis, Missouri in 1928.**
- **Died in Winston-Salem, North Carolina in 2014.**
- **Notable works:**
  - *Just Give Me a Cool Drink of Water 'fore I Diiie* (1971), poetry collection
  - *Gather Together in My Name* (1974), memoir
  - *And Still I Rise* (1978), poetry collection

Maya Angelou, born Marguerite Annie Johnson, spent most of her childhood with her paternal grandmother in Stamps, Arkansas. Although the town was very rural and racial discrimination was at the forefront of American politics, her grandmother was a well-respected member of the community. Angelou also stayed intermittently with her mother in St. Louis. However, on one of these visits, she was raped by her mother's boyfriend. After being prosecuted, the man was murdered. The trauma stemming from this event led Maya to be almost completely mute for several years.

As a teenager, Maya moved to San Francisco with her mother, where she took on a series of odd jobs, including cocktail waitress, prostitute and dancer. During this time she also became pregnant with her only child, a son. In the 1950s, Maya moved to New York City and became a member of the Harlem Writers Guild, a writing group devoted to capturing the African-American experience in literature. She also gained renown for her acting talents, even earning a Tony nomination.

Maya spent the 1960s and 1970s writing poetry, as well as her seven volumes of autobiography, which begin with *I Know Why the Caged Bird Sings*. She gained critical acclaim as one of the first authors to write truthfully and unapologetically about the African-American experience. In 1981, she became a professor of American Studies at Wake Forest University, despite her lack of college education. She composed and delivered the poem "On the Pulse of Morning" for the inauguration of Bill Clinton in 1993. In 2011 she was awarded the Presidential Medal of Freedom.

I KNOW WHY THE CAGED BIRD SINGS

A GROUNDBREAKING MEMOIR

- **Genre:** autobiography
- **Reference edition:** Angelou, M. (1984) *I Know Why the Caged Bird Sings*. London: Virago Press.
- **1st edition:** 1969
- **Themes:** race, childhood, growing up, parental relationships, discrimination, sexuality, oppression

I Know Why the Caged Bird Sings is the first in Maya Angelou's seven-volume autobiography series. It tells of her early upbringing in Stamps, Arkansas through her first few years of residence with her mother in San Francisco, following her up until the age of 17. Sometimes funny and sometimes tragic, the underlying current of the memoir is one of oppression, as a female, as an African-American, and as a child. Nevertheless, Maya's character is always sure of herself and often optimistic.

The memoir was immediately successful after its release in 1969 and earned a National Book Award nomination. Angelou was praised for her ability to write so masterfully and unapologetically about the African-American experience. The book appeared at the height of the American civil rights movement and right after the death of Martin Luther King Jr. (American religious leader and civil rights activist, 1929-1968). It marked an important moment in which the country was beginning to value and validate the experiences of African-Americans. It still stands as an important pillar of African-American literature, and indeed of literature in general.

SUMMARY

LIFE IN STAMPS

The memoir opens with Marguerite and her brother, Bailey Jr., meeting their paternal grandmother in Stamps, Arkansas after their parents have split up. Stamps is a rural town full of a racism characteristic of the American Deep South in the 1930s. Marguerite's grandmother, whom she calls Momma, is very strict and owns a general store in town. Her crippled uncle, Willie, is also a strict authority figure who makes sure that Marguerite and Bailey are properly educated. At this point in her life, Marguerite discovers a love of literature, beginning with Shakespeare.

The African-American community in Stamps endures low-level taunting as well as threats from the Ku Klux Klan. Despite this, Marguerite and Bailey learn to enjoy life in the small town and spending time at Momma's store. One Christmas, they receive presents from their parents. This is startling because they had simply assumed that their parents were dead. Soon after, their father, Bailey senior, appears in town. To the people of Stamps, he seems urbane and elegant, but Marguerite is suspicious of him. He announces that he is taking Marguerite and Bailey with him and ends up dropping them off with their mother, Vivian, in St. Louis.

LEAVING STAMPS

In St. Louis, Marguerite and Bailey Jr. move in with their mother, Vivian, and her boyfriend, Mr. Freeman. Vivian is beautiful and glamorous and Bailey Jr. immediately takes to her. However, Mr. Freeman sexually abuses and ultimately rapes Marguerite, warning her that if she tells anyone, he will kill Bailey Jr. When Vivian and Bailey Jr. discover the truth, Mr. Freeman is put on trial for his actions. He is later found murdered, most likely by Vivian's brothers. Marguerite feels terrible and somehow at fault for the entire affair. She and Bailey Jr. are then sent back to Stamps.

Marguerite believes that everyone expects her to move on from the sexual abuse incident now that she is back in Stamps. However, she is still sullen and despondent. Marguerite begins spending time with a woman named Mrs. Flowers.

Mrs. Flowers is elegant, educated and maintains an impressive status in Stamps despite being a black woman. She introduces Marguerite to poetry, urges her to communicate and helps her find her voice again.

Bailey Jr. is less pleased to return to Stamps. He misses his mother and copes with his anxiety by simulating sex with a series of local girls. Finally, he meets a well-developed girl named Joyce who convinces him to actually have sex with her. However, she ultimately leaves town and Bailey Jr. is heartbroken. He also witnesses a dark moment of racism when he sees a black man beaten to death by white men. Momma decides that Bailey Jr. and Marguerite will have a better life if they move in with their mother in San Francisco.

SAN FRANCISCO

Marguerite finds that she loves the strange charms of San Francisco and enjoys attending her new high school. She also does not mind living with her mother and her mother's new boyfriend, Daddy Clidell. She has not been there long when she is invited to visit her father and his girlfriend, Dolores, in southern California. Marguerite and Dolores take an immediate disliking to each other. This is further entrenched when Bailey announces he is taking Marguerite with him on a day trip to Mexico. In Mexico, Bailey spends his time getting drunk with loose women. He passes out in the car and Marguerite tries to drive him home, but ultimately crashes the car. After returning to California, Dolores and Marguerite have a physical altercation and Marguerite runs away. She spends the rest of the summer with a group of homeless teenagers living in cars, but ultimately returns to her mother in San Francisco.

Bailey Jr. has become a bit rebellious and decides to bring home a prostitute. His mother kicks him out of the house, and Marguerite is sad to see him go. Bored without him, she decides to become a streetcar conductor. They refuse to hire a black woman at first, but after some persistence, Marguerite finally get the job.

After reading *The Well of Loneliness* at school, Marguerite worries she might be a lesbian or a hermaphrodite (she is not sure of the difference). In order to prove she is not, she has sex with a local boy and ends up getting pregnant. She has the baby after graduating high school and cares for him with the support of her mother. In the final scene of the novel, Marguerite sleeps next to her baby and finds a sense of peace.

CHARACTER STUDY

MARGUERITE

Marguerite, sometimes nicknamed "Maya" or "My", is the narrator of the memoir. The story follows her from the age of three to the age of 17. Critics sometimes see the character of Marguerite in the story as symbolic of all black girls growing up in America. Indeed, the struggles she faces with racism and discrimination can certainly be read as universally linking her to other African-Americans. However, the particular incidents in the story and Marguerite's personal responses to them are lifted specifically from Angelou's real life.

Within the first pages of the memoir, Marguerite expresses her contempt for her own appearance, explaining how she wishes she was beautiful, blonde, and white. The reality, as she describes it, is that she is a "a too-big Negro girl, with nappy black hair, broad feet and a space between her teeth that would hold a number-two pencil" (p. 5). She is continually insecure about her looks, usually comparing herself to her cute brother.

Marguerite excels in school and has a gifted literary mind. During her time in Stamps, she is usually at the top, or second from the top, of her class. At her 8th grade graduation, she loses the valedictorian spot to Henry Reed, but she notes, "instead of being disappointed I was pleased that we shared top places between us" (p. 186). The memoir is filled with Marguerite's allusions to literature she has read and loved. She notes:

> "Although I enjoyed and respected Kipling, Poe, Butler, Thackeray and Henley, I saved my young and loyal passion for Paul Lawrence Dunbar, Langston Hughes, James Weldon Johnson and W.E.B. Du Bois' "Litany at Atlanta." But it was Shakespeare who said, "When in disgrace with fortune and men's eyes." It was a state with which I felt myself most familiar." (p. 16)

Marguerite constantly sees the events of her life through the lens of literature; she finds hope in the universality of her experience and validation by connecting that experience to literature.

BAILEY JR.

For the majority of the memoir, Bailey Jr. is Marguerite's closest and most trusted companion. As children, they play together and work together in their grandmother's store. Marguerite describes her absolute devotion to Bailey Jr., saying:

> "Bailey was the greatest person in my world. And the fact that he was my brother, my only brother, and I had no sisters to share him with, was such good fortune that it made me want to live a Christian life just to show God that I was grateful. Where I was big, elbowy and grating, he was small, graceful and smooth. When I was described by our playmates as being shit color, he was lauded for his velvet-black skin. His hair fell down in black curls, and my head was covered with black steel wool. And yet he loved me." (p. 24)

While Marguerite sees herself as awkward, she views Bailey Jr. as attractive and charming. As the pair are continually shifted between their mother, their father and their grandmother, they become each other's most constant source of love.

When Marguerite and Bailey Jr. return to Stamps after their brief time in St. Louis, Bailey is distressed about leaving his mother. Although Marguerite is glad to return to Stamps, she is still reeling from the trauma of her sexual assault. Thus, the siblings again find comfort in one another. Marguerite notes that Bailey Jr. "felt we were in the same boat for different reasons, and that I could understand his frustration just as he could countenance my withdrawal." (p. 99).

When Bailey is ultimately kicked out of his mother's house in San Francisco, Marguerite feels lost and purposeless without him. He had been, in many ways, her guiding compass. The fact that he is also mentioned in Angelou's dedication of the book is proof of their enduring bond.

MOMMA

Marguerite's paternal grandmother is credited with raising her during her most formative years. Marguerite views "Momma," as she calls her, with a deep sense of awe. She describes her with reserved admiration, saying:

> "People spoke of Momma as a good-looking woman and some, who remembered her youth, said she used to be right pretty. I saw only her power and strength. She was taller than any woman in my personal world, and her hands were so large they could span my head from ear

to ear." (pp. 50-51)

Marguerite both loves and fears Momma; she sees her as larger than life.

Momma owns a general store in Stamps which supplies both black and white customers, thus earning her a well-respected status in the community. During the Great Depression, Momma offers store credit to both the black cotton workers and white townsfolk. When Marguerite has a toothache, she recalls Momma taking her to the white dentist in town. The black dentist was far from Stamps and the white dentist had previously borrowed money from Momma. However, the dentist refuses to see Marguerite, believing that it would harm his business to treat a black girl.

Momma then sends Marguerite out and speaks to the dentist privately. Marguerite imagines a fantasy scenario in which Momma enacts her powers to banish the dentist from town. She later discovers that the dentist had simply offered to give Momma money for a bus ticket to see the black dentist. However, she notes, "I preferred, much preferred, my version." (p. 207).

ANALYSIS

AUTOBIOGRAPHY VS. FICTION

I Know Why the Caged Bird Sings is less of a direct autobiography than it is a mix of poetry and memory. The thoughts, feelings and descriptions Angelou creates often feel beyond the scope of a child's mind; thus, the experiences of a young Marguerite have clearly been enhanced by the imagination and poetic talents of an older Angelou. This interesting adaptation of the autobiographical genre is said to have resulted from Angelou's editor, Robert Loomis, challenging her to write an autobiography "as literature" (Walker, 1995: 91). Believing it was nearly impossible to write a literary autobiography, Angelou nevertheless could not resist the challenge.

Thus, the prose of the book is fuelled by poetic conventions, metaphor, imagery and allusion. Because of this, some critics have called the book "autobiographical fiction" (Lupton, 1998). Indeed, the retelling of events in the book may not always be technically historically accurate.

Angelou often rearranges events, sacrificing chronology for thematic linkings. By doing so, Angelou creates a more complete narrative and one which takes the reader on a meaningful journey rather than a simple retelling of events.

Angelou's inclusion of traditional elements of fictional literature has also been understood as her attempt to tell the story of a generation rather than simply the story of herself. Scholars such as Susan Gilbert believe that Angelou was trying to tell a collective story of the plight of African-Americans (Gilbert, 1999).

Indeed, her complex and poignant descriptions of youth and racial discrimination are clearly evocative of the American civil rights movement of the 1960s. At this point in history, there was finally a value being placed on African-American lives and African-American experience. Angelou's work was a vital part of that movement for the way it foregrounded the feelings and trials of a previously marginalised group of people.

Thus, Angelou's autobiography was more about capturing the truth in every black person's experience than it was meant to be specifically confined to her own life. Nevertheless, the nature of the autobiographical genre meant that tension between Marguerite's experience and the collective African-American experience, or the tension between autobiography and literature, is clearly present throughout the work. In many ways, *I Know Why the Caged Bird Sings* seeks to reinvent what autobiography actually is, making it more about the truthfulness of the feelings conveyed than the historical accuracy of the events. Angelou continued trying to redefine and reinvent autobiography in this way throughout her six subsequent volumes of memoir.

PARENTHOOD

The theme of parenthood acts as a frame for the events of the memoir. At the beginning of the story, Angelou emphasises the absence of Marguerite and Bailey Jr.'s parents. As she describes their train journey down to Stamps, she remarks on how other passengers must have pitied the "poor little motherless darlings" (p. 7). Vivian and Bailey's decision to send their children to Stamps leads the children to view them as non-existent, and even to eventually assume they are dead.

The question of what it means to be a parent is displayed through the different names with which Marguerite describes her different parental figures. As her paternal grandmother takes on the key role in raising her, that grandmother eventually becomes "Momma." Marguerite notes, "we soon stopped calling her Grandmother" (p. 8). Despite her not being their biological mother, Bailey Jr. and Marguerite view Momma within that central parental role.

When they are eventually brought to their real mother, Vivian, there is a sense of distance. She has not acted as a true mother to them, and for that reason they call her the formal "Mother Dear". Marguerite notes, "Bailey persisted in calling her Mother Dear until the circumstance of proximity softened the phrase's formality to "Muh Dear," and finally to "M'Deah." I could never put my finger on her realness" (p. 74). Thus, even as they become more comfortable with Vivan, she is not their "momma," and the most familiar they can ever become with her is to call her "M'Deah".

Marguerite and Bailey Jr.'s father never surmounts that barrier of distance. When he swoops into Stamps to take them away, he promptly drops them off with Vivian and then disappears. Marguerite keenly feels the absence of a father, a factor that makes her vulnerable to Mr. Freeman's advances. When Mr. Freeman sexually abuses her for the first time, initially she feels safe and wanted, believing "From the way he was holding me I knew he'd never let me go or let anything bad ever happen to me. This was probably my real father and we had found each other at last" (p. 79). The abuse scene is made all the more tragic by Marguerite's longing for a "real," father: one who would actually fulfil the fatherly responsibilities of loving her and keeping her safe.

When Marguerite herself becomes pregnant at the end of the memoir, she is afraid of being a bad parent or hurting her child in the same way that she has continually been hurt by her own parental figures. One night, Vivian tells Marguerite that the baby is to sleep in the bed with her. Marguerite fears that she will roll over and crush the baby in her sleep. However, she ultimately wakes up with the baby in her arms, safe and warm. This is a poignant moment that resolves many of the fears, tensions and anxieties about parenthood in the memoir. Marguerite's mother, Vivian, has taught her daughter how to protect her own baby, and Marguerite has learned to trust her mother and trust herself.

OPPRESSION

The title of the memoir is taken from the poem "Sympathy," by Paul Laurence Dunbar (American writer, 1872-1906). Dunbar was well known as one of the first writers to write in a black dialect and celebrate stories about distinctly African-American experiences. Both of Dunbar's parents were former slaves. Thus, the "caged bird" in his poem becomes an emblem of all African-Americans freed from the literal shackles of slavery who are still not truly free because of the rampant racial oppression and discrimination in America. Angelou's title carries all the heavy connotations of Dunbar's work.

Angelou's description of life in Stamps demonstrates the stark discrimination faced by African Americans in the South during the 1930s. When the sheriff warns Momma that Uncle Willie should hide because the Ku Klux Klan is coming out that night, Marguerite is angry about the fact that innocent men should have to hide themselves. She says, "[The sheriff's] confidence that my uncle and every other Black man who heard of the Klan's coming ride would scurry under their houses to hide in chicken droppings was too humiliating to hear" (p. 20).

In San Francisco, when Marguerite sets her heart on becoming a streetcar conductor, she is continually told that "They don't accept colored people on the streetcars" (p. 284). However, due to her perseverance she gladly reports that, "On a blissful day I was hired as the first Negro on the San Francisco streetcars" (p. 289). Thus, despite the underlying current of racial, gender-based and class-based oppression, the memoir continually fosters a sense of hope. The titular bird that stands in for the African-American people is undoubtedly caged; however, it is also singing and hopeful for a better future.

FURTHER REFLECTION

SOME QUESTIONS TO THINK ABOUT...

- How does Marguerite and Bailey Jr.'s relationship develop throughout the memoir?
- To what extent is Marguerite shielded from the dark racism of Arkansas and to what extent is she aware of it?
- How central is Marguerite's sexual assault to the flow of the memoir?
- What influence does Mrs. Flowers have on Marguerite's upbringing?
- What are the factors that lead Momma to send Marguerite and Bailey Jr. to San Francisco?
- How does Marguerite's passion for literature manifest itself in the style and content of the memoir?
- What makes Marguerite so determined to become a streetcar conductor?
- How did Angelou rise to the challenge of creating an autobiography that was also a piece of literature?
- What is the effect of Angelou's decision to title the memoir with a line from a Paul Laurence Dunbar poem?

We want to hear from you!
Leave a comment on your online library
and share your favourite books on social media!

FURTHER READING

REFERENCE EDITION

- Angelou, M. (1984) *I Know Why the Caged Bird Sings*. London: Virago Press.

REFERENCE STUDIES

- Gilbert, S. (1999) Paths to Escape. In: J. M. Braxton, ed., *I Know Why the Caged Bird Sings: A Casebook*. Oxford: Oxford University Press, pp. 104-105.

- Jaynes, G. D. (2017) Harlem Writers Guild. *Encyclopædia Britannica*. [Online]. [Accessed 16 February 2019]. Available from: <https://www.britannica.com/topic/Harlem-Writers-Guild>

- Lewis, D. L. and Carson, C. (2019) Martin Luther King, Jr. *Encyclopædia Britannica*. [Online]. [Accessed 16 February 2019]. Available from: <https://www.britannica.com/biography/Martin-Luther-King-Jr>

- Lupton, M. J. (1998) *Maya Angelou: A Critical Companion*. Westport: Greenwood Press.

- The Editors of Encyclopædia Britannica (2019) Maya Angelou. *Encylopædia Britannica*. [Online]. [Accessed 16 February 2019]. Available from:

<https://www.britannica.com/biography/
Maya-Angelou>

- The Editors of Encyclopædia Britannica (2019)
  Paul Laurence Dunbar. *Encylopædia Britannica.*
  [Online]. [Accessed 17 February 2019]. Available
  from: <https://www.britannica.com/biography/
  Paul-Laurence-Dunbar>

- Walker, P. A. (1995) Racial Protest, Identity
  Words, and Form in Maya Angelou's I Know Why
  the Caged Bird Sings. *College Literature.* 22(3),
  pp. 91-108.

ADDITIONAL SOURCES

- Andrews, W. L. et al. (1997) *The Oxford Companion
  to African American Literature.* Oxford: Oxford
  University Press.

- Baisnée, V. (1997) *Gendered Resistance: The
  Autobiographies of Simone de Beauvoir, Maya
  Angelou, Janet Frame and Marguerite Duras.*
  Amsterdam: Rodopi.

- Braxton, J. M., ed. (1999) *Maya Angelou's I Know
  Why the Caged Bird Sings: A Casebook.* Oxford:
  Oxford University Press.

- Challener, D. D. (1997) *Stories of Resilience in
  Childhood: The Narratives of Maya Angelou, Maxine
  Hong Kingston, Richard Rodrigues, John Edgar
  Wideman, and Tobias Wolff.* New York: Garland
  Publishing.

- Evans, M. et al. (1985) *Black Women Writers: Arguments and Interviews*. London: Pluto.

ADAPTATIONS

- *I Know Why the Caged Bird Sings*. (1979) [Film]. Fielder Cook. Dir. USA: Tomorrow Entertainment.

www.brightsummaries.com

Ebook EAN: 9782808018616

Paperback EAN: 9782808018623

Legal Deposit: D/2019/12603/97

Cover: © Primento

Digital conception by Primento, the digital partner of
publishers.

Made in the USA
Monee, IL
06 April 2023

31448937R00026